MrSCATTE[R'S]
MAGIC SPELL

Jackie Vivelo
with
illustrations by
Margaret
Chamberlain

DK

DORLING KINDERSLEY

LONDON • NEW YORK • STUTTGART

A DORLING KINDERSLEY BOOK

First published in Great Britain in 1994
by Dorling Kindersley Limited,
9 Henrietta Street, London WC2E 8PS

A CIP catalogue record for this book is
available from the British Library

ISBN 0-7513-7015-0

Acknowledgements
The author would like to thank:
Barb Marinak, Reading Specialist, and the students of
West Hanover Elementary, Harrisburg, Pennsylvania,
who offered comments and suggestions.

The teachers and staff of
Wharton Elementary School, Lancaster, Pennsylvania,
whose "secrets" convinced me to write the story.

Colour reproduction by DOT Gradations
Printed in Singapore

Everyone in Mr Scatter's class liked
Mr Scatter, even though lessons were
confusing at times.

Peter Scatter was an absentminded
teacher. Sometimes he forgot what
he was going to say halfway through
a sentence.

While taking the register one morning Mr Scatter began, "Jean Cooper, Mark Downey, Tom For ... For ..."

Tom Fordham waited expectantly, until at last Mr Scatter continued, saying, "Four times nine is thirty six, five times nine is forty five, and six times nine ..."

His pupils had to remind him to dismiss the class at the end of the day. Once he dismissed the class, but forgot to go home himself and they found him asleep at his desk the next morning. The best times were when he didn't call them in from break.

One morning Mr Scatter came to school wearing one roller skate and one slipper. On another day, he tried to use a banana to clean the chalkboard.

Once he forgot he was talking about trade routes to China and told the class, "So after many years in the Far East, Marco Polo returned home … returned home …" Then softly, as the last echo of "returned home" died away, they heard him begin to sing, "Home, home, on the range."

You never knew what might happen when Mr Scatter was teaching.

"What was it we were studying?" he asked one day.

"It's time for the magician," Tom told him.

"Of course, magic! We'll have a lesson on the history of magic."

The class groaned. They couldn't let Mr Scatter make them miss another special assembly!

A few minutes later, Mr Scatter's class took their seats facing the stage.

WHERE IS MR SCATTER?

HE PROBABLY FORGOT WE WERE ON OUR WAY TO THE MAGIC SHOW AND WENT TO LUNCH INSTEAD.

YEAH! MR SCATTER IS PROBABLY SITTING ALL ALONE IN THE CANTEEN RIGHT NOW.

Mr Scatter **was** all alone, but he wasn't in the canteen. He sat in front of a lighted mirror in a small dressing room behind the stage. He carefully applied glue to his face and stuck on a long, bushy, pointed beard.

Next he covered his short blond hair with a dark wig. He pulled on a tailcoat and dropped a black cape with a red silk lining over his shoulders. Then he carefully placed a top hat on his head.

9

Swirling his cape, he
bowed to the mirror.

"Mr Scatter,"
he said, "meet the
Magnificent Scarlotti!"

Mrs Poppenberry, the head teacher,
poked her head through the door.

"Are you ready?" she asked. "Yes, I can
see you are. I'll introduce you."

Mrs Poppenberry walked on to the stage. For today's magic show, she wore a smart red dress. Looking out at the audience, she said, "I'm pleased to introduce the wonderful, astounding, sensational – Magnificent Scarlotti!"

Everyone clapped as the curtains
opened to reveal a bearded man in a
top hat with a long, red-lined cape.
The dashing magician flashed a
dazzling white smile.

With a flourish of his left hand, the
Magnificent Scarlotti pulled a bouquet
of purple and yellow and orange
flowers from the air. As the audience
looked at them in wonder, the
flowers burst into flames.

"Now," said the Magnificent Scarlotti, in a gravelly voice, "I will saw someone in half. May I have a volunteer from the audience?"

Every hand went up, but the magician chose Mrs Poppenberry. He locked Mrs Poppenberry into a box with her head showing at one end and her feet at the other.

The Magnificent Scarlotti waved a saw above his head and then began to saw the box containing Mrs Poppenberry into two pieces.

"The box is now separated into two sections," the Magnificent Scarlotti told the children. He pushed one half to one side of the stage and the other half to the opposite side. Mrs Poppenberry turned her head to look at the children. Mrs Poppenberry's feet wiggled.

"Are you all right, Mrs Poppenberry?"

"Yes, yes, but you're wrinkling my dress! Put me back together."

"Of course. Watch as we bring Mrs Poppenberry back together."

The Magnificent Scarlotti removed his top hat and bowed low. He stood up slowly, looking at his hat. All the children looked at the Magnificent Scarlotti and his hat.

At last the Magnificent Scarlotti said, "For my next magical, marvellous, mysterious trick, I will pull a dozen rabbits from …

MY EMPTY HAT!"

He twirled the hat to show that nothing was inside.

He pushed up his sleeve, then reached into the hat with his bare hand, and pulled out a large, bright red goose egg with white stars on it.

One after another he pulled out a purple duck egg, a blue and yellow egg, and a tiny orange egg.

"One! Two! Three! Four!" he counted. "Keep watching! We'll find a full dozen."

He pulled out a small green and black striped egg.

"Number five!" the audience chanted.

"Number six!" they shouted as a large magenta egg appeared.

The Magnificent Scarlotti held the egg up high. Everyone waited, ready to shout, "Number seven." But the magician just stood staring at the egg. Finally, with a twitch of his long pointed beard, he turned to the audience.

"My seventh trick!" he cried. "For my seventh trick, I will make this drum disappear!" The magician tapped his hat and the magic hat turned into a drum.

The confused children mumbled.

The Magnificent Scarlotti swung his red-lined cape off his shoulders and dropped it over the drum.

"Now, when I count to three, I will remove the cape and the drum will disappear."

"Where are the rest of the eggs?" asked someone in the second row.

"Get me out of here!" called
Mrs Poppenberry's head. But the
Magnificent Scarlotti wasn't listening.
He was carefully arranging the folds
of his cape.

"Say the magic words with me,"
he told the audience.

"Put me back together!"
Mrs Poppenberry demanded.

"No! No!" the Magnificent Scarlotti
said. "**Those** aren't the magic words.
Repeat after me:
Simon, flymon, ginger beer,
Hurcus, spurgus, DISAPPEAR."

Instead of pulling the cape away, the
Magnificent Scarlotti looked at the
children. He stared at Mr Scatter's
class. For a moment all was silent.

"For my final trick, I will make an elephant appear right here on the West Humbug School stage."

"You didn't make anything **disappear** yet," someone reminded the magnificent magician.

The Magnificent Scarlotti was
wheeling a huge box on to the stage.

He pushed it in front of
Mrs Poppenberry, in front of the
hat and eggs, in front of the drum
covered with the red-lined cape.

"The box is empty," the magician
pointed out, "but watch carefully!"

The Magnificent Scarlotti began
folding in the sides of the box,
until only the back was left. Then
he pushed the last partition off the
stage, crying, "SOCKO!"

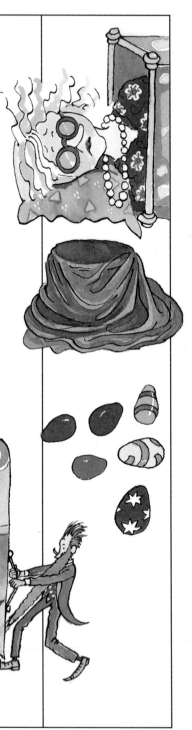

There on the stage was an elephant
with a magician's cape draped
over his back.

Everyone applauded.

Mrs Poppenberry yelled, "Help!"

The elephant trumpeted.

HELP!

The Magnificent Scarlotti began to bow, then seemed to forget what he was doing and wandered off the stage.

All the children whooped and clapped and shouted and whistled and stamped, but the Magnificent Scarlotti didn't come back.

When they were sure he wasn't coming back, some of the children tried magic words of their own.

ABRACA-POCUS HOCUS-CADABRA!

ZIG, PIG, POP, PUM!

DULA, DABA, BONGA, SHONGA, SNUFF!

IG-LA ZIG-LA BIG-LA BE!

Slowly the children drifted out of
the hall. No one knew what to
do about Mrs Poppenberry or
the elephant.

When Mr Scatter's class returned to their room, they found their teacher waiting for them.

"You missed it," Joe told him. "The Magnificent Scarlotti was, well, magnificent!"

"Maybe we should continue our lesson on the history of magic," said Mr Scatter. "Now let's see. The oldest written record of a magic show is from Ancient Egypt. Egypt was ruled by a pharaoh, who was something like an emperor. The emperor …"

"Umm, the Emperor Napoleon was defeated at the Battle of Waterloo."

OH NO, MR SCATTER. NOT WATERLOO, MAGIC.

DO YOU KNOW ANY MAGIC WORDS, MR SCATTER?

"Magic words," echoed Mr Scatter. "Oh, of course, the magic words! Repeat them with me everyone!"

SOCKED OUT! ROCKED OUT! ROCKO! SOCKO!

A haze of purple smoke filled the classroom. Everyone, including Mr Scatter, began to cough. As the air slowly cleared, the first thing everyone saw was an elephant; the elephant from the magic show.

On the cape on the elephant's back sat Mrs Poppenberry, the head teacher, looking surprised. On her lap was a large nest of bunnies, at least a dozen rabbits, all oddly coloured. One rabbit was red with white stars. Another one was green and black. These were not like any rabbits the class had seen before.

The drum had disappeared, but a bouquet of purple and yellow and orange flowers was tucked behind the elephant's ear.

The elephant trumpeted.
Mrs Poppenberry opened her mouth and yelled. The children clapped.

"Everything is here except Scarlotti!"
Mark pointed out.

"He probably made himself
disappear," said Tom.

"An invisible magician! What a
great trick! This is much better
than a boring lesson on magic,"
said Patty.

"It's too bad Mr Scatter didn't get
a chance to see Scarlotti, so he'd
know what a **real** magician is like,"
added Sophie.

Mr Scatter scratched his head and
tried to remember what he had
been teaching. The elephant reached
out with his trunk and grabbed
Mr Scatter's yellow hair, which he
had pulled into peaks on top
of his head.

"The elephant!" Mr Scatter exclaimed
as the big animal tugged his hair.
"Some elephants," he explained to the
children, "come from India, but the ones
with the biggest ears come from Africa.
This one," he said, happily pointing to
its large ear, "is an African elephant!"